WILLIAM
~ HEADS TO ~
HOLLYWOOD

INTERNATIONAL CAT OF MYSTERY

HELEN HANCOCKS

This book is dedicated to my grandma, with love and thanks

First U.S. edition 2016

Library of Congress Catalog Card Number pending
ISBN 978-0-7636-8913-1

16 17 18 19 20 21 TLF 10 9 8 7 6 5 4 3 2 1

Printed in Dongguan, Guangdong, China

This book was typeset in Baskerville Old Face.
The illustrations were done in pencil and gouache.

TEMPLAR BOOKS
an imprint of
Candlewick Press
99 Dover Street
Somerville, Massachusetts 02144
www.candlewick.com

WILLIAM
HEADS TO
HOLLYWOOD

HELEN  HANCOCKS

templar books
an imprint of Candlewick Press

William, international cat of mystery, was bored.
Recently, all his cases had been easy to solve.

Just the other week, he had to find a missing hat,
which turned out to be on the client's head.

William was beginning to despair
of ever cracking another major case . . .

when a perfumed letter
arrived for him.

It was from Audrey Mieowski,
the loveliest star in Tinseltown!

Dear William,

*I need your help!
The statues for the Golden
Cuckoo Awards have been
stolen, and the ceremony is
tomorrow night. It's a highly
suspicious case, and you are
the cat to solve it.*

*Don your detective hat
and meet me at the airport.*

Yours,

Audrey
Mieowski

This was the case he'd been waiting for.
William was heading to HOLLYWOOD.

Audrey met him at the airport.
She was even more dazzling than
in her films.

"There's no time to lose,"
she said. "The Golden Cuckoos
are the most important awards
in Hollywood."

They sped off to Cuckoo Studios—the scene of the crime.
"There were ten statues," explained Audrey, "and now they're all gone!"

William searched the scene for clues.

He found a hairpin . . .
and some blue feathers.

"These could be the leads we need to catch the thief!" exclaimed William.

The hunt was on.

But first William needed lunch—a case was never solved on an empty stomach.
They headed to the studio cafeteria.

As they were finishing, in burst Ms. Vivienne Baxter, once the greatest star of them all.
"You must be the cat who is investigating the crime of the stolen statues. Who could do
such a thing? I wish you luck, Mr. William." And out she swept.

"That's strange," said Audrey.
"She's never even talked to me before.
Something fishy is going on. Let's be in
cahoots and crack this case together!"

It didn't take them long to find
more blue feathers. . . .

"These feathers aren't the ones from the crime scene," said William. "They're much too long."

But up ahead was a set of footprints . . .

STAGE 12

STAGE 14

that led the sleuthing cats straight onto the set of the latest Cuckoo Western.

CUT !

William was so busy following the footprints that he ran into a rack of costumes.

"Aha!" he cried. "We've found our first statue."

"These costumes came straight from the props department," said Audrey.

"Then that's our next stop."

The props department
was crammed with treasures.

William gazed around, spellbound.
How would they ever find
anything in here?

After hours of searching, William and Audrey
were no closer to finding the rest of the Golden Cuckoos.
"Oh, fish sticks!" William exclaimed.

"Never give up," said Audrey.
"There's a big costume party before the Golden Cuckoo Awards tonight.
Let's mingle with the stars and see if we can discover the culprit."

William had never seen anywhere so grand and palatial.

He was also highly impressed
with the canapés, and was just about
to order milk—frothed, not stirred . . .

when in walked
Vivienne Baxter.

There was something
familiar
about her outfit.

The feathers in her scarf matched those at the crime scene . . . and the decoration in her hat looked like . . .

a Golden Cuckoo!

"She's the thief!" William shouted.

Ms. Baxter looked up in alarm and fled.

Audrey and William set off in hot pursuit . . .

speeding down the Hollywood Hills . . .

across Sunset Boulevard . . .

all the way out to the Santa Monica Pier.

DONUTS

"Quick, there she is!" cried William. "Heading into the hall of mirrors."

But she had vanished!
"Let's take the Ferris wheel for a
better view," suggested Audrey.

From up high,
they could see Ms. Baxter
running to the end
of the pier.

DONUTS

"There's nowhere left to run!" they shouted as they raced after her.
"We know it was you."

STOP!
STOP!

"Yes," she cried. "I stole them all! But I deserved them.
And if I can't have them, no one can."

NooooOOoo!!!

With those words,
she flung the statue into the sea.
Bravely, William leaped in after it.

"Oh, William," said Audrey as she tossed him a life preserver. "How heroic!"

"All I wanted was recognition," confessed Ms. Baxter. "No one ever appreciated me. And if you cats must know, the other eight are stashed at my mansion."

"I just wanted to be perfect!" she added as the police came to take her away.

William and Audrey raced to the mansion.
"At last," said William. "We've cracked this case."
And just in time . . .

CUCKOO AWARDS

CUCKOO AWARDS

for the Golden Cuckoo Awards
to take place, with William
as guest of honor.

At the end of the ceremony, William was presented with an award of his very own—

the Golden Cuckoo for Best Cat Detective of the Year.

All too soon, it was time for William to bid Audrey farewell.

They both agreed it had been a beautiful partnership.

William's time in Hollywood was over . . .

or was it?